Dear Parents and Teachers,

In an easy-reader format, **My Readers** introduce classic stories to children who are learning to read. Although favorite characters and time-tested tales are the basis for **My Readers**, the books tell completely new stories and are freshly and beautifully illustrated.

My Readers are available in three levels:

1 **Level One** is for the emergent reader and features repetitive language and word clues in the illustrations.

2 **Level Two** is for more advanced readers who still need support saying and understanding some words. Stories are longer with word clues in the illustrations.

3 **Level Three** is for independent, fluent readers who enjoy working out occasional unfamiliar words. The stories are longer and divided into chapters.

Encourage children to select books based on interests, not reading levels. Read aloud with children, showing them how to use the illustrations for clues. With adult guidance and rereading, children will eventually read the desired book on their own.

Here are some ways you might want to use this book with children:

- Talk about the title and the cover illustrations. Encourage the child to use these to predict what the story is about.
- Discuss the interior illustrations and try to piece together a story based on the pictures. Does the child want to change or adjust his first prediction?
- After children reread a story, suggest they retell or act out a favorite part.

My Readers will not only help children become readers, they will serve as an introduction to some of the finest classic children's books available today.

—LAURA ROBB

Educator and Reading Consultant

For activities and reading tips, visit myreadersonline.com.

To Aurora and Marigold
—M. H.

An Imprint of Macmillan Children's Publishing Group

Printed in China by Toppan Leefung, Dongguan City, Guangdong Province.
For information, address Square Fish, 175 Fifth Avenue, New York, NY 10010.

Library of Congress Cataloging-in-Publication Data Available

ISBN 978-1-250-01044-5 (hardcover)
1 3 5 7 9 10 8 6 4 2
ISBN 978-1-250-01015-5 (paperback)
1 3 5 7 9 10 8 6 4 2

Book design by Patrick Collins/Véronique Lefèvre Sweet
Square Fish logo designed by Filomena Tuosto

First Edition: 2013

myreadersonline.com
mackids.com

This is a Level 2 book

Lexile 470L

The Wind in the Willows

A Fine Welcome

Susan Hill · illustrated by Michael Hague

inspired by Kenneth Grahame's *The Wind in the Willows*

SQUARE FISH
Macmillan Children's Publishing Group
New York

Mole lived deep underground
in a dark, cozy house
called Mole's End.
One fine day,
something was different.

Maybe it was how the birds chirped,
or the sun shined,
or the wind blew,
but something made him
dare to go up.

So Mole left Mole's End

and started walking.

Soon he came to the river.

He saw a Water Rat sitting in a boat.

“Hello,” said the Rat.

“Do you have a rhyme for *river bank*?”

Shy Mole blinked.

"*Draw a blank*?" Mole said.

"That will do," said Rat.

"Will you ride in my boat?"

Mole blinked at the boat.

“I wouldn’t dare,” said Mole.

He blinked again.

“But just this once, I’ll try,” he said.

Mole stepped into the boat.

He rocked, then sat.

He smiled at Rat.

“Excellent!” said Rat.

"Do you have a rhyme for *excellent*?"

asked Rat.

Mole scratched his nose.

"*Heaven sent*?" said Mole.

"That will do nicely," said Rat.

Suddenly the water bubbled.

Up came Otter.

“Join me for a swim!” said Otter.

“Gladly,” said Rat.

He slid into the water.

“Help!” cried Mole.

“Row!” said Rat.

“I wouldn’t dare!” said Mole.

But Rat and Otter went under the water and didn’t hear.

Mole took up the oars.
"Just this once, I'll try," he said,
and he began to row.

Soon Rat and Otter

waved from the river bank.

“Over here, Mole!” said Rat.

Mole waved back

and almost lost an oar.

“Oh my!” cried Mole.

He rowed to the bank.

“Well done,” said Rat.

“Do you have a rhyme for *well done*?”

“*Jolly fun*!” Mole said.

“This calls for a picnic,”

said Rat.

Just then Toad and Old Badger came by.

"A party!" Toad cried.

"I never miss a party!

What is a party without me?"

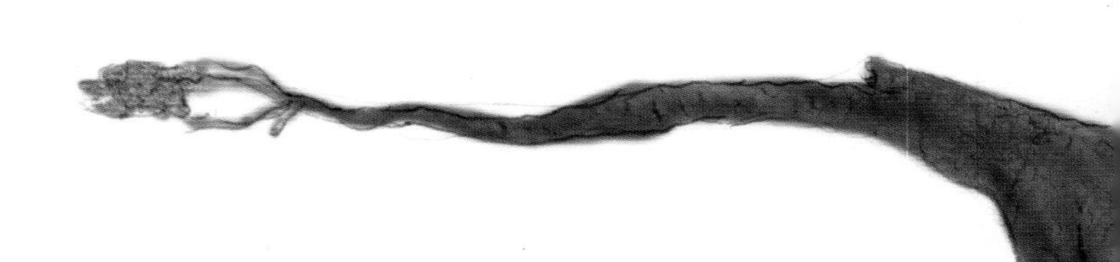

"Dear Toad, dear Badger,
meet Mole," Rat said.
"I have no time for picnics,"
said Old Badger, "but here I am.
I will make the best of it.
Kindly pass the pickles."
Rat said to Mole,
"Do you have a rhyme for *pickles*?"
"I have no rhyme for *pickles*," Mole said.
Mole leaned back and laughed.
He leaned so far that . . .

. . . the basket fell into the water!

In an instant,

Mole jumped into the river

to grab the basket

before it was swept away.

At last Mole came up dripping wet
and gave the basket to Rat.
“Brave Mole!” said Rat.
“You might have drowned!” said Toad.
“I surprise myself,” said Mole.
“Today I am daring to do
more new things than I ever knew!”
“Good rhyme, Mole!” said Rat.

The friends ate every last bite
of every last thing,
and Mole ate the last pickle himself.
"Now I will read my poem," said Rat.

"Welcome, Friend,

three cheers I send

to you for all of your daring.

River bank, draw a blank,

excellent, heaven sent,

well done, jolly fun—

Pickles!"

Rat looked around at his friends.

"Not my best poem," he said,

"but I mean every word of it."

"Thank you, Ratty," said Mole.

"It's a fine welcome."

Mole smiled at his new friends.

Something was different.
Maybe it was how the birds chirped,
or the sun shined, or the wind blew,
or how his friends smiled back.

But something made him think he'd stay.